Hooray for Our Heroes!

D0211852

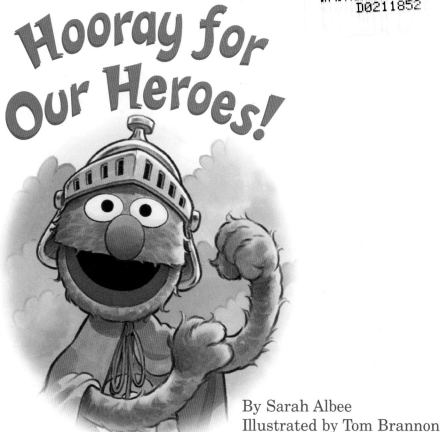

By Sarah Albee
Illustrated by Tom Brannon

"Sesame Workshop"®, "Sesame Street"®, and associated characters, trademarks, and design elements are owned and licensed by Sesame Workshop. ©2002, 2010 Sesame Workshop. All Rights Reserved.

The DALMATIAN PRESS and PIGGY TOES PRESS names and logos are trademarks of Dalmatian Publishing Group, Atlanta, Georgia 30329. No part of this book may be reproduced or copied in any form without written permission from the copyright owner. All rights reserved.

Printed in Dongguan, Guangdong, China

10 11 12 13 SF 36041 10 9 8 7 6 5 4 3 2 1
Sesame Street Handle Box Set Book: Hooray for Our Heroes!

Hello there, everybodee! It is I, your furry superhero pal, Super Grover! Today I am going to tell you what the word "hero" means. A hero is someone who you see in comic books and cartoons. Heroes are make-believe.

First of all, a hero has a special uniform, similar to the outfit that I am wearing, with a cape on the back and a letter on the chest. I do not see anyone else wearing a hero uniform, do you?

And, of course, everyone knows that heroes have very large muscles and are very strong. No one around *here* is especially strong.

Heroes move with lightning speed. No one around *here* can do that.

Of course, heroes must also be able to fly. Aside from yours truly, no one around *here* can do that.

And heroes must be able to leap tall buildings in a single bound.

Heroes are famous. They are never the people that we see walking around our own neighborhoods.

How would you know a hero if you saw one? That is a very good question! And I, Grover, will answer it for you. For starters, heroes definitely do not wear glasses.

And heroes do not just sit around, waiting for things to happen.

Heroes rescue people who need help. I do not see anyone around here being rescued, do you?

Heroes are people you look up to.

I hope that now you understand what it means to be a hero. Thank you!